Here Comes the Bride

D1321722

Katie Price's Perfect Ponies

1. Here Comes the Bride
2. Little Treasures
3. Fancy Dress Ponies
4. Pony Club Weekend

HERE COMES THE BRIDE
A BANTAM BOOK 978 0 553 82074 4

First published in Great Britain by Bantam,
an imprint of Random House Children's Books
A Random House Group Company

This edition published 2007

1 3 5 7 9 10 8 6 4 2

www.randomhouse.co.uk/paper.htm

Set in 14/21pt Bembo MT Schoolbook

Bantam Books are published by Random House Children's Books,
61–63 Uxbridge Road, London W5 5SA

www.**kids**at**randomhouse**.co.uk
www.rbooks.co.uk

Addresses for companies within The Random House Group Limited
can be found at: www.randomhouse.co.uk/offices.htm

THE RANDOM HOUSE GROUP Limited Reg. No. 954009
A CIP catalogue record for this book is available from the British Library.

Printed in the UK by
CPI Bookmarque, Croydon, CR0 4TD

Katie Price's Perfect Ponies

Here Comes the Bride

Illustrated by Dynamo Design

Bantam Books

Vicki's Riding School

Vicki

Jess and Rose

Cara and Taffy

Amber and Stella

Sam and Beanz

Mel and Candy

Henrietta and President

Darcy and Duke

Chapter 1

Jess buried her face in Rose's silver mane. "You're the most beautiful pony in the world!" she whispered.

Jess still couldn't believe how lucky she was. Not only was she a regular helper at Vicki's Riding School; she was also the

yard girl in charge of Rose, a lovely grey
Connemara pony. A year ago Jess had had
her first riding lesson at Vicki's and overnight
her world had turned upside down. She had
loved the lesson and the stables, and now
she just couldn't get enough of ponies! Small
ones, fat ones, naughty ones, nervy ones,
even cheeky ponies – they were all brilliant.

Jess knew her mum would never be able
to buy her a pony of her own, not unless she
won the lottery! Mum hardly earned enough
to keep Jess, her brother and herself going.
But by doing a bit of overtime she scraped
together enough money for Jess to have a
riding lesson every other week.

Luckily for Jess, there were other girls
just like her at Vicki's Riding School. They
were Jess's age and they all loved ponies, so
she had quickly made friends with them.
Clever Amber, with her deep dark eyes and
long black hair, was now Jess's closest friend.

2

Amber was so sensitive that she seemed to understand exactly what the ponies were trying to say. Then there was ginger-haired, freckly Sam, who was the joker of the group; skinny Mel, who was already an amazing show-jumper; and pretty little Cara, with big eyes and long blonde hair, who was a nervous rider but never gave in to her fears. None of these girls owned a pony either but they were all pony mad!

When Vicki told Jess and her friends that she'd give them extra lessons if they helped her out at the stables, they jumped at the deal. Now they could spend all their free time down at the riding school, mucking out, sweeping the yard and grooming the ponies.

Vicki had given each of the girls a pony to look after. Jess was given Rose, who she loved more than anything in the world. Amber looked after gentle Stella, the black Highland pony with a white blaze. Mel firmly handled Candice, the chestnut Arab (who everybody called Candy). Frisky Beanz, the skewbald New Forest cross, was just right for scatty Sam. And calm little Taffy, the palomino Welsh with his thick creamy golden mane and tail, was perfect for timid Cara.

Vicki had two other ponies stabled at the riding school: she had learned to ride on them and couldn't bear to part with them. Greedy little Dumpling, a dark bay Shetland, and a light bay Dartmoor pony called Flora. Vicki also had her own stunning three-day-event mare, Jelly, a chestnut Irish-cross thoroughbred who had qualified for Badminton the year before.

A sharp nudge in the tummy brought Jess out of her daydream. Rose tossed her head and neighed loudly.

"Sorry, sweetheart, I was miles away," giggled Jess.

She bent to get the hoof pick out of the pink plastic tack box at her feet. It was her own tack box – she had saved up for months to buy it. Jess had decorated it with pink pony stickers, pink ribbons and a big pink bow.

"Foot up," she ordered.

Rose patiently lifted up one hoof at a time so that Jess could clean out the dirt and mud.

"Let's make you even more beautiful," said Jess.

"Rose looks pretty gorgeous already," said a voice behind her.

Jess turned to see Vicki, the owner of the riding stables, standing at the open stable door. Jess secretly hero-worshipped Vicki. She was everything Jess wanted to be when she grew up. Tanned and slim, with thick dark hair and stunning silver-grey eyes, she always looked amazing. Vicki was living proof that you could work with horses and still be glam. Even in muck-stained jeans and a grubby hoodie, she always managed to look good, although she often had to work a fifteen-hour day.

As owner of the riding school, Vicki had to turn her hand to everything. She mucked out the stables, hosed and swept down the yard, groomed the ponies, took care of the tack, washed the horse blankets, tidied the muck heap, gave riding lessons and ran the office. Without Vicki's kindness Jess wouldn't have Rose to take care of. Vicki always said it was a fair swap in return for Jess's hard work. What Vicki didn't know was that she had made Jess the happiest girl in the world.

Vicki opened the stable door and patted Rose's shimmering silver coat. "You've done a lovely job on her," she said.

"I've been grooming her for more than an hour," Jess said shyly.

Rose pushed at Vicki's jeans pockets. Every pony in the yard knew that soft-hearted Vicki always carried mints around with her.

"Greedy girl!" she joked and ran a hand along Rose's silky mane. "She's as shiny as my earrings. Well done, Jess."

Jess smiled proudly. She'd told Vicki she'd
been grooming Rose for an hour. In fact it
was nearly three! She didn't mind though.
Making Rose look beautiful was the best
thing in the world. Picking out her feet,
oiling her hooves and combing out her thick
silver tail . . . None of it felt like work!

Vicki gave Jess the packet of
mints and she held one
out on the flat of her
hand and offered
it to Rose. The
pony snuffled
loudly as she
took it, then
crunched it
noisily between
her teeth. "Let's

hope Rose doesn't roll in the mud before her
first lesson," Vicki said, grinning.

Jess laughed. "She'll probably be covered in mud after her jumping lesson with the twins anyway," she said.

The twins, Bill and Ben, were the youngest riders in the yard. They were sweet but very noisy, and always arrived full of energy. They loved jumping in the outdoor school, but Rose usually came back covered in sweat and mud after they'd ridden her, and Jess had to start grooming her all over again.

"You might have to look after the twins next week," said Vicki.

"Won't you be teaching?" Jess asked.

Vicki shook her head. "I'm going to be chief bridesmaid at my best friend Sarah's wedding."

Jess's green eyes widened. "What, Sarah who helped out with lessons last year?"

"Yes, that's right. She's marrying a famous show-jumper and they've asked me to be their bridesmaid. I've been friends with

Sarah since we were six and started having riding lessons together."

"Wow! Have you got a posh dress?"

Vicki nodded. "Fuchsia-pink silk, fuchsia-pink satin shoes and fuchsia-pink roses in my hair!"

"You'll look beautiful," said Jess.

Vicki frowned. "I'm really worried about leaving the ponies for the day though," she said. "Saturday is our busiest time and it's a lot to ask of you girls – to look after the place on top of all your other jobs here."

"Don't worry," said Jess. "Susie will keep an eye on us."

Eighteen-year-old Susie was the oldest of the helpers and had a BHSI qualification. When Vicki wasn't around, she took charge. Sometimes, if Susie was in one of her moods, she acted like she knew it all. But she always put the ponies first, which was why Vicki trusted her.

"Oh, I know," said Vicki, "but I haven't been away for a whole day for ages and I reckon I'm really going to miss the ponies."

Jess laughed. "It's only one day. Honestly, we'll take really good care of the place and the ponies."

"I know," said Vicki. "It's just me being an idiot."

Just then the clang of the yard gate bashing against the wall made them both jump.

"Nine o'clock," said Vicki, then added with a laugh, "First lesson of the day – let's get a move on!"

Jess and her friends led the beginner riders round the yard while Vicki gave them their lesson.

"Bottoms down. Knees in!" she called out.

Jess was leading Bill on Rose. The pony was good with children but sometimes got impatient with their over-enthusiasm. Little Bill yanked too hard on her reins and Rose stopped dead in her tracks.

"Trot on!" yelled Bill excitedly.

But Rose wouldn't move. She whinnied loudly and shook her head.

"She's telling you to show some respect!" Jess said.

"What's *respect*?" Bill asked.

"Treating her nicely. Try to handle her gently – and don't yell at her so much," Jess replied. "I bet you wouldn't like it if somebody kept yanking at your mouth and shouting at you."

Bill grinned. "Sorry, Rosie," he said. Then, firmly but gently, he pressed his heels into the pony's side. "Trot on," he said softly – and this time Rose did!

Clip-clop, clip-clop, clip-clop. All round the yard she went, with her silver mane lifting in the breeze.

"Well done, Bill and Rose," Vicki called out as they passed by. She winked at Jess as if to say, Well done for teaching Bill some manners!

All through the lesson Jess was thinking about Vicki. She wished she could make it easier for her to be away from the ponies next Saturday. She'd do anything to make Vicki happy. She'd love to see her glammed-up as a bridesmaid, walking behind the bride and groom. But no way was that going to happen. Vicki would be at the church; Jess and her friends would be looking after the ponies. Then Jess had a wicked idea. Perhaps there was a way of looking after the ponies, making Vicki happy and seeing her as a bridesmaid too . . .

Chapter 2

The lessons finished at twelve but Jess liked
to spend quality time with Rose after her
morning's work. First she made sure the
pony got a bucket of cool fresh water,
then she took off her saddle and bridle and
brushed her down before turning her out
into the meadow where all the other ponies
were grazing. Jess unclipped the lead rope
attached to Rose's head collar and gave her
a gentle pat on the neck.

"Off you go, babe," she said.

Rose threw back her pretty head and
neighed loudly. Jess leaned against the
five-bar gate and smiled as the other

ponies trotted up to meet her. Taffy sniffed
Rose's nostrils and Candy blew in her
ears. Rose snorted, and with a little kick
of her back legs she trotted off. The other
ponies followed, and before long they were
all wildly chasing each other around the
meadow. Jess smiled at them.

She could have spent hours watching the ponies but her rumbling tummy reminded her that she was hungry. Apart from an apple which she'd shared with Rose she'd had nothing to eat since six o'clock that morning. Jess ran back to the yard and joined her friends in the tack room.

Amber, Sam, Cara and Mel were stuffing their faces with food from their packed lunches.

"Phew! What a morning," said Amber.

"Want a cheese roll, Jess?" asked Sam.

Jess shook her head. "No thanks. I've got some ham ones in my bag. I'm dying for a drink though. I get well thirsty grooming Rose."

The girls sat round an old wooden table covered in cans of drink and crisp packets. Curly-haired Mel, with a banana in one hand and a biscuit in the other, swung backwards and forwards on two legs of her chair. She wasn't scared of anything when she was on Candy, and she could ride faster and jump higher than any of the other girls.

"Be careful, Mel," warned Cara, who was always concerned about people hurting themselves.

"Don't worry about *her*," joked Sam. "If Mel hurts herself, then it's her own fault. And I'll nick her crisps."

The others laughed. Then, as they swapped biscuits and fruit, Jess told them about Vicki being a bridesmaid at Sarah's wedding.

"You know what?" she said with a big grin on her face. "I think we should surprise Vicki. We could ride over to the church and show her that the ponies are OK. And we'd get to see a bit of the wedding too!"

Amber put down her sandwich and looked thoughtful. "How are we going to do that?"

Jess took a big gulp of her drink. "Well, I've been thinking . . ." she said.

"That must have been an effort!" Sam teased her.

Jess screwed up an empty crisp packet that was lying on the table and chucked it at her. "Shut up and listen to my plan," she said, laughing.

Cara's big blue eyes twinkled with excitement. "Go on, Jess," she begged.

"Well, the wedding's at two in the afternoon," Jess began.

"And riding lessons here finish at twelve," Mel added.

Jess nodded. "That gives us two hours to get the ponies ready and walk over there," she said.

"How long will it take us to get over there?" Sam asked.

Mel turned to Amber. "We rode over that way to a show-jumping competition about a month ago," she said.

"It took about three quarters of an hour," Amber remembered.

Jess clapped her hands. "So we could just make it."

"As long as there are no problems on the way over," said Amber.

Cara grinned. "Imagine Vicki's face when

she walks out of the church and sees us lot all waiting for her," she said.

"Hey! We could form a guard of honour," said Amber.

"What's that?" asked Mel.

"It's like an archway that the bride and groom walk under," Amber explained.

"Cool!" cried Jess. "We could sit on our ponies and hold up our riding whips. That sounds perfect for the wedding of a riding instructor and a show-jumper."

Cara was so excited she started jumping up and down. "Let's decorate our whips with pink ribbons so they match Vicki's bridesmaid's dress," she said.

Amber burst out laughing. "Yeah, let's put pink ribbons on the ponies' bridles too," she suggested.

"And we should all wear pink," said Jess.

"Yuk! I hate pink," said Mel, who was a bit of a tomboy.

"Tough!" said Sam. "We all like it and so does Vicki."

"OK, OK," said Mel. "If I have to, I have to. I'll borrow something off my cousin Tina."

Jess jumped up. "This is going to be cool!" she shouted.

"Wicked!" laughed Sam as she chucked a dandy brush up in the air.

"I hope that's not *my* brush," called a voice from the tack-room door.

At that sound all smiles faded.

The voice belonged to Henrietta Reece-Thomas, the snootiest girl in the yard.

"Actually it's *my* dandy brush," Sam said quickly.

"Well, make sure you don't mess around with any of my stuff," Henrietta replied.

Unseen by Henrietta, Sam pulled a funny face which made Jess laugh. Henrietta was such a pain! She was one of the livery girls who paid top money to stable their ponies at Vicki's yard. She owned President, a fabulous spotty grey Appaloosa who'd been shipped over from the States by her parents as a surprise birthday present for their little princess. Grumpy Mr Reece-Thomas ran a big computer company and had so much money he didn't know what to do with it! They lived in a house ten times bigger than Jess's. They had a garden with a pool, sports cars and a yacht. But Henrietta was always in a mood and her dad was the rudest man Jess had ever met.

23

"Who did the bedding in President's box this morning?" Henrietta demanded.

"Me," Amber replied.

"Well, next time make it deeper," Henrietta barked. "My father doesn't pay all that money for you to be tight with my pony's bedding."

Amber clenched her fists angrily. "I wasn't being tight with President's bedding," she replied. "Vicki told me to go easy on the straw because we're getting low. We'll be able to top it up this afternoon when the delivery comes."

Henrietta's eyebrows shot up. Without another word she stomped off, her nose in the air.

"Bossy cow!" giggled Mel.

"Just because she owns the most expensive pony in the yard doesn't mean she can treat us like dirt!" said Jess angrily. "Just ignore her, Amber. She's not worth it."

Henrietta was always picking on Jess and her friends and looking down her nose at them. A few of the other livery girls in the yard could be a bit snobby but none of them were as mean as Henrietta. Jess had actually made friends with one livery girl called Darcy; she said that Henrietta was rude to everyone. Darcy owned a beautiful dark bay show-jumper called Duke. She wasn't one of their group but Jess liked her and she seemed to like Jess.

"You're right. I'm not fussed about Henrietta!" said Amber as she reached up to the shelf where the riding hats were kept.

"Anyway, we've got other things on our minds," said Jess as she grabbed her hat too. "Like the fact that we've only got a week to practise our guard of honour!"

Chapter 3

Later that afternoon, while the girls were tidying the muck heap, they tried to work out a plan. As they shovelled the steaming stuff out of a wheelbarrow, Mel said, "It'll be impossible to practise while Vicki's around."

"Yeah, she might guess what we're doing," said Sam.

Cara stopped work and wiped her forehead. "We can't just tack up the ponies and take them into the field without Vicki's permission," she said anxiously. "She'll go mad if she catches us."

"That's the risk we'll have to take, Car," Jess told her. "If we ask Vicki's permission, we'll have to give her an explanation."

"And that'll give the secret away," added Amber.

Jess leaned on the yard brush she was using and wound her thick brown hair around her fingers – it was something she often did when she was thinking hard. "So we've got no choice but to go behind Vicki's back," she said.

"How can we find out when she's not going to be around?" Sam asked.

"We could check in the office diary," suggested Amber. "You know – the one Vicki uses for booking the riding lessons."

Jess immediately leaned her brush against the wall and said, "Good idea. I'll go and look now."

Luckily the office was empty so Jess could check the diary easily. Five minutes later she was running back to her friends. "Vicki's in this afternoon but she's out on Sunday, Wednesday and Thursday afternoons, then she's in the yard all day Friday," she told them.

Amber's dark eyes twinkled. "Cool! It's Sunday tomorrow. We'll start then," she said.

The following afternoon, as soon as Vicki drove off in her old Jeep, the girls tacked up their ponies and walked them

29

over to the meadow. Unfortunately they passed President's stable on the way there. Henrietta bobbed her head up over the top of the stable door and glared at them.

"What are you doing?" she snapped.

All five girls froze in their tracks. This was all they needed – gobby Henrietta snooping around after them. Quick-witted Amber was the first to speak. "We're just warming up the ponies for a lesson," she lied.

Henrietta came out of the stable with her eyes narrowed. "Well, I hope you've asked

Vicki's permission," she said.

Mel, who hated Henrietta even more than the other girls did, pressed her heels into Candy's slender chestnut side. "Of course we have," she replied. "You don't have to know everything that's going on around here," she added, and she cantered off without another word. The other girls followed straight away, leaving Henrietta looking daggers at them.

"I hope she doesn't go and tell Vicki," Cara said as she dismounted to open the gate to the meadow.

"Don't worry, Daddy will be picking Henrietta up just as soon as he's finished his round of golf!" Sam said in a voice that sounded just like grumpy Mr Reece-Thomas.

"And if we're lucky, we won't see Henrietta for the rest of the afternoon," Mel added.

Jess didn't want to waste any time worrying about Henrietta. "Come on, she's not worth it. Let's get started," she said. "We've got loads to do before Vicki gets back."

"Jess, we need an even number of riders if we're going to do the guard of honour right," said Amber. "It'll look weird with an odd number of us. We all need a partner."

"You're right," said Jess. "Five of us

won't make much of an arch. I should have thought of that. Let's ask Darcy – you know, that livery girl I've been talking to? She's well nice."

Mel, Cara, Sam and Amber looked doubtful.

"She's not one of us," said Mel.

"She's *way* too posh to be one of us," joked Sam. "She's got her own pony."

"She's a livery girl," Amber reminded Jess, "not a yard girl."

Cara's pretty face looked thoughtful. "Jess is right though. Darcy's nice," she said. "She's not like Henrietta!"

"And she's got a lovely pony," said Jess.

Nobody could argue with that. Duke was the best pony in the yard at jumping against the clock.

So the girls agreed that Jess should go back to the stables and ask Darcy to join them.

Darcy was a plain-looking girl but she had the longest brown hair Jess had ever seen. It was always in a plait which dangled down her back. Jess often wondered what Darcy did with it when she was riding. Did she sit on it or tie it to the saddle?

When Jess told Darcy about the wedding and asked whether she wanted to join them, she agreed straight away. She looked up from grooming Duke and grinned.

"It sounds fun," she said. "I love surprises."

Jess dropped her voice to a whisper. "Don't mention it to anybody else," she said. "Especially Henrietta." She nodded her head towards President's stable, which was next door to Duke's.

Darcy winked. "I won't tell anyone," she answered in a low voice.

"We're going to dress up, and do the ponies too," Jess told her. "Wear something

34

pink and bring lots of pink ribbon for
dressing up Duke."

Darcy laughed excitedly. "I could use it to
plait up his mane and tail," she said. "And I'll
wear my pink silk over my riding hat."

"Cool," said Jess. "I'm saving up for a pink
silk, but at the rate I'm going I won't have
one till next year!"

"I've got an *old* pink silk," Darcy said.
"You can have that if you like."

Jess's green eyes widened in surprise.
A pink silk, even if it was old, would be
amazing. "Really? Wow! Yes please!" she said.

"I'll bring it with me on Saturday," Darcy
promised. "But I can't practise with you now
because my mum's picking me up in a few
minutes. We're going to my gran's for tea."

"What about Wednesday or Thursday?"
asked Jess.

"No, sorry. I don't finish school as early as
you do. We have to stay on to do prep," she
said.

Jess laid her head against Duke's warm
neck and listened to the steady rhythm of his
breathing. She giggled when he blew into
her hair.

"You've got nothing to worry about," she
told Darcy. "Duke's a real gentleman – he
won't put a foot wrong. It's us lot that have
the frisky ponies and need the practice! We'll
just talk you through it on the way over to

the church on Saturday. See you then."

Jess was right. Rose, Stella, Beanz, Candy and Taffy were very frisky. They fidgeted and played up as the girls practised their guard-of-honour line-up for most of the afternoon. The tighter they pulled in their reins, the more the ponies resisted.

"We're not getting anywhere. Let's take them for a gallop around the meadow to calm them down," said Amber, who was always quick to sense the ponies' moods.

Cara looked scared. "I've never galloped before," she said in a nervous voice.

"Don't worry, Car," Jess reassured her friend. "Taffy would never run off with you."

"Last one to the five-bar gate is a loser!" said Sam, laughing as she shot off on Beanz.

"Cheater!" shouted Mel as she pressed her heels firmly into Candy's side. It was all the pretty chestnut Arab needed. Tossing her silky mane, she kicked up her back legs and opened out into a breathtaking gallop.

"We'd better catch up with them," said Amber.

"We'll be lucky," replied Jess.

Steady Stella broke into a brisk trot while Rose, encouraged by Jess, galloped after Candy and Beanz, who were now almost at the gate.

Cara was the last to arrive, her face flushed with excitement.

"That was amazing!" she shouted as she patted Taffy's blond mane.

Mel chuckled as she stroked Candy. "Yeah, galloping is wicked!" she said.

Sensing her rider's excited mood, Candy reared up. But tough Mel could keep her seat on any horse. "Whoa there, girl," she said as she reined her in. "Right, you've had your fun – now we've got work to do."

The girls were so busy they didn't notice Henrietta Reece-Thomas spying on them from behind a bush. She really wanted to find out what Vicki's "little helpers" were doing while she was away. She really should let Vicki know what they were up to, she thought.

The exercise did help to make the ponies settle down and do what they were told. Cara and Darcy led the line-up on Taffy and

Duke, the middle couple were Amber and Mel on Stella and Candy, and Sam would be at the end with Jess on Beanz and Rose.

"Duke should calm all the ponies down," said Amber.

"I hope so!" replied Mel, laughing as Candy tugged at her reins.

Jess checked the time on her watch. "Come on, we've got to get this guard of honour right before Vicki gets back," she said.

As the girls joined whips above their heads, Amber eyed the space underneath. "Will Sarah and her husband have enough room to walk under our arch?" she asked.

"As long as they're not giants it'll be fine," Sam decided.

"We've got to keep the ponies still for at least five minutes," Jess said.

Cara laughed shyly. "The bride won't be pleased if they trample all over her long white dress," she said.

But as the girls concentrated hard on holding up their whips, they suddenly saw Vicki striding into the field with Henrietta at her side. Her pretty tanned face was set in an expression that Jess had never seen before. She looked furious! Jess's stomach flipped in fear. How could she have been so stupid as to risk upsetting the woman she hero-worshipped? Her heart raced and she felt her skin grow hot and clammy.

"Just what do you think you're doing?" Vicki demanded.

All five girls had dropped their whips to their sides and were wriggling awkwardly in their saddles. The ponies instantly caught their mood and started to toss their heads and paw the ground.

"And who gave you permission to take the ponies out?" Vicki asked sharply.

"We, er . . ." Jess dismounted quickly, she couldn't think of anything to say – she certainly didn't want to lie to Vicki. Her face went bright red as she blurted out, "I'm sorry, we should have asked you first."

Vicki's silver-grey eyes swept along the line of girls, who all looked embarrassed. What if she banned them from the riding school? Jess thought in despair. Even worse, what if Jess never saw Rose again? She fought back the tears that were flooding into her eyes.

"Take the ponies back to their stables immediately," Vicki snapped. "I thought I could trust you girls, but obviously I can't. I was worried enough already about leaving you in charge on Saturday with Susie, but now I'm dreading it. I'm very disappointed in all of you." And giving a last glare at the girls, she walked away.

With a big smirk on her face, Henrietta watched the girls trot back towards the yard.

"Cow!" muttered Jess furiously under her breath.

Chapter 4

That was the end of any practice. The
girls didn't dare take the ponies out again.
Whenever they had a few moments alone,
they each tried steadying their pony and
raising their whip, but it wasn't really
enough – and it certainly wasn't the same as
all getting together and making an arch.

Before and after school for the rest of the
week the girls worked extra hard to prove
to Vicki that they were reliable and that she
could trust them to look after the place on
Saturday.

On the morning of the wedding, Amber
and Jess were the first to arrive at the yard.

They cycled in wearing their old jeans
and sweatshirts, and hung up the clothes
they were going to
change into later,
carefully hiding
them under their
coats. Jess had
brought a pink
riding jacket. Amber
had a bright pink
blouse and a
pink belt decorated
with dangly silver bits.
They'd both got lots of pink
ribbon for their ponies' bridles
and for themselves too.

"What's up, Jess?" Amber asked as her
friend anxiously twirled her hair around her
fingers. "You don't seem as excited as you
were earlier in the week."

Jess pulled down the corners of her

mouth. "I *am* excited," she said. "But I'm really worried. We've not practised enough. Our guard of honour could be total rubbish and then we'd ruin the wedding instead of making it extra special!"

Amber put her arm round her. "There was no way we could have risked another practice session. We were dead lucky that Vicki didn't kick us out for using the ponies without asking in the first place. Maybe when she leaves for the wedding, we can have another practice before we go."

Jess picked up her riding hat from the shelf by the door and frowned. "I don't think there'll be time, Amber. There's so much to do here first, and then we've got to get changed and dress up the ponies. And with Vicki away, Henrietta is bound to be spying on us, ready to tell tales.'

Amber grabbed her hat and crammed it over her dark hair. "Then we'd better

47

make sure that Susie says it's OK to take the ponies out this afternoon," she said.

"I tried asking her yesterday but Vicki turned up and I had to change the subject," Jess told her.

Amber opened the tack-room door. "Come on, let's find Susie before the lessons start," she said.

As they walked across the yard to the office, Cara arrived carrying her change of clothes in a plastic bag in one hand. In the other she held a beautiful wreath of fresh flowers. When she saw her friends staring at the wreath, she blushed.

"I hope you don't mind," she stuttered nervously. "I thought I might give this to the bride and groom from all of us. It's kind of like a little wedding present."

Jess grinned. "Oh, that's so sweet, Car," she said.

Cara smiled as she skipped towards the

tack room. "I'm going to hang it up in here," she said with a laugh. "As far away from the ponies as possible."

Just then the office door opened and Susie stepped out.

"Can we have a word please, Susie?" Jess asked.

"Make it quick," Susie snapped. "I've got a double workload with Vicki being off today."

Jess dropped her voice to a whisper. "Actually it's about Vicki," she said. "We're planning a surprise guard of honour for Sarah's wedding."

Susie looked blank. "What's that got to do with me?" she asked.

Amber took a deep breath. "Well, you see, we planned to ride over to the church on the ponies," she blurted out.

"Why?" asked Susie.

"Because Vicki's going to be missing the ponies and because we want to do something special for Sarah on her wedding day. She's always really nice when she comes to visit Vicki and help out at the stables."

Susie slapped her riding whip against her leather boots. "How many of you are going?" she asked.

Jess held up her hands and ticked off the names on her fingers. "Me, Amber, Cara, Mel, Sam and Darcy on Duke," she said.

"So you'll want five ponies?" Susie said.

The girls nodded and held their breath as they waited for the reply.

Please don't say no, Jess thought.

Susie suddenly started marching off towards the yard. The girls jogged along behind her, waiting for her answer. "OK, you can take the ponies," she said. "Vicki's definitely worried about leaving them today. I reckon if she sees them and hears that the morning lessons have gone well, she'll probably have a better time at the wedding reception. But remember, the ponies will have had a busy morning, so don't overwork them in the afternoon."

The girls punched the air with their fists.

"Yessss!" cheered Amber.

"Oh, thank you," said Jess, relieved.

"You're going to have to work for it," Susie said smartly. "Get the ponies tacked up – it's nearly nine o'clock."

As the girls ran off towards the stables, grumpy Mr Reece-Thomas came driving into the yard in his massive silver four-wheel drive. When he saw Susie, he turned off the engine and got out of the car. Henrietta quickly jumped out too.

"My daughter tells me that it's you in charge this morning," he barked at Susie.

She was so shocked by his loud voice that she turned as white as a sheet. "That's right. Vicki will be out at a wedding," she replied politely.

"I do not pay good money to have my daughter supervised by an inexperienced young stable hand!" Mr Reece-Thomas yelled.

Blood flooded back into Susie's cheeks as she struggled not to yell back. "I am *not* inexperienced," she started to say, but then, to everybody's amazement, the door of Vicki's cottage opened and Vicki stepped out in a gorgeous pink strapless silk dress.

"Is there a problem, Mr Reece-Thomas?" she asked as she glided down the garden path looking like a model.

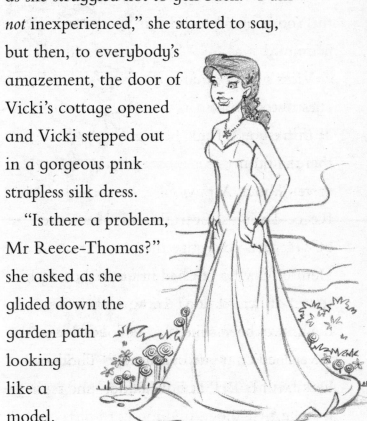

Mr Reece-Thomas's mouth dropped open at the sight of beautiful, elegant Vicki, her long hair tied up in a French pleat and decorated with pretty pink flowers.

"I'm concerned about the lack of staff here this morning," he said grumpily.

Vicki's silver-grey eyes rested on him. "I think you'll find there's nothing to worry about, Mr Reece-Thomas. Everything's taken care of." Her ice-cold gaze then moved on to Henrietta, who blushed bright red as Vicki stared at her. "I don't know what your daughter's been saying to you, but I would never leave my yard unsupervised. Susie here has her BHSI qualification and is a trained first-aider, and my yard girls are all well trained and very responsible." And then she turned on her pink satin high heels and walked up the garden path with her pink silk dress floating around her.

"Wow! She's so cool!" Jess muttered to Amber.

"She definitely told him where to shove it!" Amber agreed.

Looking a bit embarrassed, Mr Reece-Thomas got back into his four-wheel drive and roared off, leaving Henrietta standing alone in the yard. When she saw the angry expression on Susie's face, she rushed off as fast as she could. Susie muttered under her breath as she scowled after Henrietta.

"Little minx!" she said.

Five minutes later, Bill and Ben arrived for their lesson in a very bad mood.

"I want to ride Rose today," said Ben crossly.

"It's my turn!" yelled Bill.

The two little boys started to fight.

"You always ride her!" shouted Ben as he grabbed Bill's mop of thick red hair.

"Liar!" Bill shouted back as he tried to kick his brother on the shin.

"Stop it, you two," said Susie. "I don't need this," she said to Jess. "Not today of all days. I don't know how Vicki copes with these two normally. They're so naughty."

Jess was used to naughty boys. Her six-
year-old brother, Charlie, was always either
causing trouble or in the middle of it. He'd
got even worse since their dad left, and Jess
had got used to handling his bad moods.
If she saw that Charlie was about to have
a tantrum, she always tried to make him
laugh, especially if Mum had just come
home tired after a hard day's work at the
supermarket.

"It's OK, Susie. Leave them to me," she
said. She took hold of Bill and Ben and
held them firmly apart so that they couldn't
fight. "Who rode Rose last week?" she
asked.

Bill dropped his head and looked sulky.
"I did," he muttered.

"So it's Ben's turn to ride Rose today,"
said Jess. "And it's your turn to ride
Dumpling, Bill," she added firmly.

But even Dumpling, the cute little

Shetland pony who was a brilliant jumper, didn't bring a smile to Bill's face. He heaved himself up, still frowning, and trotted around the indoor school, slumping in his saddle.

"Sit up, Bill," Susie called sharply. "You look like a sack of potatoes!"

Five minutes later Bill excused himself.

"Can I go to the toilet?" he asked.

Susie looked annoyed. The toilet was next to the office in the yard, quite a long walk from the indoor school. Bill would have to ride there on Dumpling – otherwise he'd miss almost half his lesson.

"Make sure you tie Dumpling up while you're in the toilet," she called after Bill as he trotted off.

Jess and her friends set up the jumps; this was always the favourite part of the lesson. It was only after Ben had finished jumping a clear round on Rose that Jess looked around for Bill. Where was he? She hurried off in search of him and found him sulking in the feed room.

"Where's Dumpling?" Jess asked.

Bill shrugged. "I left her outside."

"Did you tie her up?" Jess asked quickly.

Bill shook his head and mumbled, "No, I forgot."

Jess felt like shaking him. "That's really naughty, Bill," she said as she dashed to the door. "Dumpling could be anywhere!"

Luckily Dumpling hadn't trotted out of the yard; instead she'd been wandering around looking for something tasty to eat. As she trotted past the tack room, she'd smelled something fresh and flowery so she'd poked her head in over the bottom half of the door. Dumpling had neighed happily when she saw the sweet-smelling flowers dangling from the coat hooks nearby. Jess found the greedy Shetland with her head over the door, chewing on the last of the daffodils and tulips. Her relief at finding Dumpling safe and well turned to horror when she saw what the pony was eating.

"Oh, no!" Jess wailed. "Cara's wedding wreath!"

Bill got told off by Susie, who said that if he behaved badly again, he wouldn't be allowed back into the riding school! Bill said he was sorry, but nothing made up for the fact that the wreath was wrecked. Cara tried hard not to cry but everybody could see how upset she was.

"Dumpling's such a greedy pig!" Mel fumed.

"Oh, but I hope she doesn't get colic," said Cara, who still worried about the ponies even when she was upset.

"She deserves to have a tummy ache," said Sam crossly.

Amber defended the little Shetland. "You shouldn't blame Dumpling. It's Bill who caused the problem in the first place," she said.

"It doesn't matter who we blame – Cara's wedding wreath's gone," said Jess.

Darcy had come over to join them after the riding classes finished. "If we got some more flowers, we could make a new wreath," she suggested.

Jess looked quickly at her watch. "We haven't got time to pick flowers. We've got to be out of here in an hour," she said, "and none of us are anywhere near ready yet."

Darcy smiled and winked at her. "Maybe I can get somebody to pick flowers for us," she said.

Feeling tense and under pressure, Jess threw up her arms. "Whatever!" she said. "But right now we've got to get these ponies ready."

The girls tied the five ponies up outside their stables, which ran in a line along the yard. Luckily none of them were really muddy so grooming them didn't take too long. The hard bit was fixing the ribbons to their bridles. Candy hated having the fluttering pink things close to her eyes so Darcy suggested Mel put ribbons in the pony's beautiful chestnut mane.

Rose didn't mind being dressed up at all; in fact she quite liked it, and the pink of the ribbons brought out the shimmering silver in her thick coat. Stella and Taffy, who were

both very laid-back, didn't bat an eyelid
when Amber and Cara put ribbons on their
bridles, but Beanz wasn't having any of it!
He tossed his head and shied away from
Sam, who was having a complete sense-of-
humour failure after he had stamped on her
toes twice.

"He won't let me near him," Sam
grumbled.

"Why don't you tie the ribbon to your saddle then?" Jess suggested. "He won't see it but it'll still look well nice."

"Good idea," said Sam.

When the ponies were ready, the girls rushed into the tack room to change into their clean clothes. Darcy was already dressed. She was wearing a pink jumper and had put a pink ribbon in her long dark plait that exactly matched the ribbon she'd woven into Duke's mane and tail.

"I'll stay with the ponies to make sure they don't nibble each other's ribbons," she said.

Even though they were all working against the clock, the girls could hardly get changed, they were laughing so much. Jess looked glam in her pink jacket, and Darcy's old pink silk really finished it off. Amber's shocking-pink blouse went well with her pink belt, which was thickly decorated with jingling silver pendants.

"You sound like Beanz when he's chomping on his bit!" joked Sam, who was wearing a pink bomber jacket and putting pink ribbons in her spiky ginger hair.

"Nobody will see them under your riding hat," Mel pointed out.

Sam shrugged, smiling. "Who cares? They still look cute!"

Mel looked brilliant in pink jeans that were so tight she could hardly bend down.

"They'll split in half when you mount up!" said Jess.

"That's OK – I've got pink knickers underneath!" giggled Mel.

Cara looked cute as usual in a pink T-shirt with a glittery star on it.

They were all a bit surprised when they heard a knock on the tack-room door.

"Oh, no! I bet it's Henrietta," spluttered Cara. "I mucked out President for her. I've probably done something she's not happy with."

Mel pushed Jess towards the door. "Go and open it," she said.

"Why me?" Jess asked.

"Because you're the nearest one to the door," Mel replied.

"Only because you pushed me!" Jess laughed.

They all let out a sigh of relief when Jess nervously opened the door and they saw that it was only Darcy's mum.

"Sorry to bother you," she said, "but can I borrow the ruined bridal wreath for a few minutes?"

The girls just looked at each other as Cara handed it over.

"Thanks," said Darcy's mum as she took the wreath and shut the door behind her.

Cara looked confused. "What's she going to do with it?" she asked.

Jess checked her watch for the millionth time. "I haven't a clue, but if we're not out of here in ten minutes, we aren't going to make the wedding."

After they'd tied pink ribbon to their riding whips and hats, the girls legged it into the yard, where they got the biggest surprise of their lives. While they'd been changing, Darcy's clever mum had re-made the bridal wreath with spring flowers, all picked from her own garden.

"I rang Mum on my mobile," Darcy explained. "She does all the flowers at church so I knew she could knock up a wreath quickly."

"I thought these would look really pretty in your riding hats," said Darcy's mum as she gave each of them a tiny posy made from pink carnations.

"Wow! Thanks!" said Jess.

After Darcy's mum had clipped the posies onto their hats, the girls finally mounted up. Cara put the new wreath round her neck. "I don't want Taffy nibbling it on the way there," she said, giggling.

They waved goodbye to Darcy's mum and trotted out of the yard in a long line. Car drivers waved at the procession of ponies wearing fluttering pink ribbons.

Sam started singing at the top of her voice.

Jess turned to Amber and grinned. "Phew! I never thought we'd make it."

Amber grinned back at her best friend. "We're not there yet!" she said.

Chapter 5

Worried that they'd be late for the wedding, Mel started taking a short cut, jumping over hedges and gates – which the other ponies couldn't do.

When Amber saw Candy's flaring nostrils and heaving sides, she said, "You'd better slow down, Mel. Candy's getting well excited and we're not even halfway there."

Mel reined Candy in tightly. "We're late," she pointed out. "We've got to get a move on."

Candy's high spirits quickly spread to frisky Beanz, who shot off down the bridleway. Candy reared up and even Mel, who had a grip of iron, couldn't hold her back. The lively Arab broke away and took off down the track after Beanz.

Amber sighed and shook her head. "Good one! Now we've got two over-excited ponies," she said.

Cara peered anxiously down the bridleway. "I hope Mel and Sam are all right," she said.

Darcy, who was in the lead on Duke, said, "I'll go and see where they are." And she galloped off too, but not as wildly as Mel and Sam.

Jess, Amber and Cara caught up with them at the end of the bridleway and were relieved to find Candy and Beanz much calmer after stretching their legs. In a quieter mood they trotted down a winding country lane lined with banks covered in daffodils and yellow primroses. At the end of the lane was a single-track bridge which Jess called Tremble Bridge because it shook when anybody walked over it. Jess halted Rose and turned to her friends.

"The bridge feels scary when it wobbles but it's quite safe," she told them.

Sam, who wasn't good at heights, pulled a face. "Great! One day somebody will say that and then the bridge will fall down with them on it!"

Cara looked down at the gurgling river flowing underneath the bridge. "Let's

hope that doesn't happen today," she said
nervously.

"Is this really the only way we can go?
I can't see Beanz liking a wobbly bridge,"
said Sam.

"It's the quickest way," said Jess. "We haven't got time to go around by the main roads. Honestly, stop worrying, Sam, it's fine. See?" she said, and she led the way on Rose, followed by Darcy on Duke and Amber on Stella.

"It's OK, babe," Amber said softly as sensitive Stella's dark ears went back. "We'll soon be on the other side."

Reassured by Amber's gentle voice, Stella whinnied and crossed the bridge, which wobbled as Cara set off on Taffy. Cara looked scared stiff but little Taffy just shook his long flowing creamy mane and trotted across without a sideways glance! Cara's blue eyes glowed with pride as she joined her friends on the other side.

"Taffy's such a star!" she said as she bent to put an arm about his warm neck.

Then the trouble started. Beanz got halfway across the bridge, then stopped dead in his tracks and started to toss his head.

"Come on, gorgeous," urged Sam, but Beanz neighed nervously and showed the whites of his eyes. "He's scared!" she yelled to her friends. "I knew he would be."

"Get off and walk him across," Amber suggested.

Sam slowly dismounted and took hold of Beanz's reins, but no coaxing would shift him.

Amber jumped off Stella and handed her reins to Jess. "Hold onto her," she said, and set off across the bridge to help Sam.

When she reached Beanz, Amber held out her hand so that the pony could smell the mints she had cupped in her palm. She rubbed Beanz's soft white nose and whispered, "You can have as many mints as you want if you cross the bridge, boy."

Amber then turned her back on Beanz and walked away from him. Smelling the packet of mints still in her hand, Beanz snorted greedily and quickly trotted after her.

"Clever boy!" cried Sam as she ran along beside him.

Once on the other side Amber gave Beanz a big kiss and half a packet of mints. As he crunched them, he kept nudging Sam in the tummy.

"I think he's trying to tell me to carry mints for the next emergency," Sam joked. "Thanks a lot, Amber."

Mel was the last to set off, though it would have been better if she'd gone first. Candy had waited too long on the other side and now she was seriously spooked by the bridge.

"She won't move!" Mel yelled across to her friends.

No matter how much she tried to persuade the sensitive little Arab, Candy would not budge – even mints didn't seem to help.

"You'd better go without me," Mel shouted to her friends. "If I ride fast, maybe I can go round and take the main roads to the church."

"No way!" they all shouted back.

"Not even *you* could ride that fast," said Amber. "You'll *never* get there in time."

Jess looked at the river gurgling under the bridge. "If you could get down the riverbank, you could easily cross the river," she shouted to Mel.

Cara went white. "Isn't that dangerous?" she gasped.

Amber shook her head. "Mel's the best rider out of all of us," she said. "She could go up and down Mount Everest without falling off!"

"And the water's really shallow anyway," Darcy added.

Jess clicked her tongue and steered Rose towards the riverbank. "I'm going down there," she said. "Candy might be calmer if she can see one of us on the other side of the river."

Cara looked scared. "Don't!" she cried,

but Rose was already in the shallows, dipping her head to drink the water that flowed around her hooves.

Candy neighed excitedly when she saw Rose. Eager to join her, she jumped down the bank and landed in the water with a splash!

"Aaahhh, that's freezing!" Mel laughed as cold water flew up into her face and soaked the ribbons in Candy's flowing mane.

Tossing her head, Candy trotted quickly across the river, which never came higher than her chestnut hocks. When the two ponies met up, they squealed excitedly and nuzzled each other. Candy sprang forward and leaped onto the riverbank, which was now muddy under their hooves. Jess and Mel giggled at the playful ponies.

"They're having fun," said Jess as Candy pushed in front of Rose and started up the bank.

"Whoa!" cried Mel as she clung onto Candy's neck.

Not to be outdone, Rose scrambled up the riverbank too. Jess clutched her thick silvery mane to stop herself from falling.

"Help!" she cried as she wobbled in her saddle.

Candy jumped to the top of the bank, but as she did so, she sent up a spray of mud which flew out behind her. Splat! It hit Jess and Rose, who were directly behind.

"Ugh!" yelled Jess as big blobs of dirty black mud splattered her face and pink jacket. Rose was covered in mud too – it dripped down the pink ribbons attached to her bridle onto her chest and legs.

"That's the last time I'll help a friend out!" Jess said as she wiped mud off her mouth.

When she rejoined her friends back on firm ground, they all helped to clean her up, especially Mel, who kept apologising.

"I'm so sorry," she said over and over again.

"Don't worry," said Jess, then stopped as she heard a sound that made her heart sink. "Church bells!" she gasped. "What time is it?"

Amber quickly checked her watch. "Oh no! It's half past two!" she gasped. "They'll be coming out of the church any minute."

So, covered in mud, Jess joined her friends in a breathtaking gallop across the open fields that led to the church, from where the sound of bells rang out.

Chapter 6

As the ponies neared the church, Jess realized that the bridal party inside would be sure to hear their thudding hooves. Waving her arms in the air, she managed to get her friends' attention.

"Slow down!" she mouthed rather than shouted.

All the girls pulled their ponies up and dismounted. As they walked them along the grassy path that led to the church porch, Taffy and Beanz snatched at the spring flowers lining the way.

"Stop that, greedy guts," Sam told Beanz, who looked funny with a red tulip poking out of the corner of his mouth!

Suddenly the girls heard organ music booming out, so they quickly remounted and took up their positions – Cara and Darcy by the door, Amber and Mel in the middle, with Sam and Jess at the end. But on the one afternoon they'd practised they hadn't been as nervous as they were now. The ponies, except for calm little Taffy, were quick to pick up their mood. Candy's nostrils flared, Rose tossed her muddy silver mane, Beanz snorted, Stella stamped her feet and even Duke fidgeted restlessly.

Amber had soon handed out mints to the ponies, which at least took their minds off bolting. The girls regrouped just as the church doors were flung wide open and the bride and groom came out, smiling broadly. Taking deep breaths to steady themselves, the girls held up their pink-ribboned riding whips in their left hands and grabbed their reins tightly in the right.

The look of amazement on the faces of Sarah and her new husband was nothing compared to the expression on Vicki's.

She gasped as she stepped out into the churchyard: there were her ponies, neatly lined up, with pink ribbons fluttering from their saddles and bridles! The girls beamed as the bride and groom walked under their perfect guard of honour. When they came out at the other end, the guests were waiting for them with handfuls of rice and confetti.

"Congratulations!" they shouted as they chucked confetti over the couple.

As Sarah and her new husband posed for the photographer under an apple tree, Vicki patted and cuddled each of her ponies in turn.

"You all look so beautiful," she said.

Tossing the muddy pink ribbons in her bridle, Rose blew into Vicki's hair.

"What happened to you, sweetheart?" Vicki asked.

Jess grinned. "Candy got spooked by

Tremble Bridge so Rose and me had to rescue her," she said.

"And then Candy splattered them both with mud," Mel added.

Vicki patted Rose, who started to nibble her bridesmaid's bouquet. "I don't know how you managed to do all the morning lessons and this too," she said.

"With difficulty!" Jess laughed. "We had a terrible morning."

"And a terrible journey getting over here," Sam added with a giggle.

The photographer waved at them. "We need you over here, Vicki," he called out.

"And the ponies too!" Sarah added.

Feeling a bit shy, the girls trotted over and joined the guests, but the ponies weren't in the slightest bit embarrassed. Beanz nibbled the wax flowers on one lady's hat while Candy helped herself to a man's buttonhole.

Just as the photographer was taking
a romantic photograph of the bride and
groom kissing each
other, Taffy popped
up between
them and
neighed at
the top of
his voice.
Everybody
was roaring
with laughter
when the camera flash
went off. Even Jess, covered like Rose
in blobs of black mud, was laughing her
head off!

Before they left, Sarah and her husband
thanked the girls for organizing such a
wonderful surprise.

"We'll make sure you get some wedding
cake," Sarah promised.

The wedding car drew up and more pictures were taken, which gave Vicki a few more moments to talk to the girls.

"I think I owe you an apology," she said. "I've just realized that you were practising in the field when I told you off."

The girls nodded. "We couldn't explain or it would have spoiled the surprise," Amber said.

"We felt bad that we'd gone behind your back but we really didn't have any choice," Jess blurted out.

Vicki shook her head and looked guilty. "I'm sorry. Henrietta gave me some story about you jumping the ponies all afternoon. I should have known better than to listen to her," she said.

The girls nodded their heads again, very firmly.

"At least we managed to surprise you," said Sam.

"And the photographs should be brillliant," Mel added.

'Especially the one of Taffy with the bride and groom," said Jess.

As the wedding party drove away, Vicki called out of the open car window, "Have a safe journey home!"

The girls waved until the car was out of sight, then Jess threw her riding whip up in the air.

"Yeah! We did it!" she yelled.

"Yeah!" all the other girls shouted, and their whips went high in the air too.

"I still can't believe it," said Amber. "Everything that could have gone wrong went wrong but we still got here."

"It was worth it just for the look on Vicki's face when she walked out and saw us," said Mel.

The happy smile slowly faded from Cara's pretty heart-shaped face. "I'm dreading the journey back," she admitted.

Sam made a worried face. "Ugh! The Terrible Tremble Bridge!" she giggled.

"Can't we go the other way home?" Cara asked nervously.

Amber shook her head. "It's a really long way round and I don't think we should take the ponies on the main road without Vicki or Susie here," she said.

Mel quickly mounted up. "Let's get a move on then," she said. "I don't want to be stuck on that stupid bridge in the middle of the night."

Chapter 7

The ponies trotted along happily. They were tired and ready to get home. As they approached Tremble Bridge, Jess crossed her fingers, which was difficult because she was still holding onto her reins.

"I'm going first this time," said Mel, and putting Candy on a tight rein she urged her forward.

Everybody was pleased when Candy briskly trotted across the bridge. She was soon followed by all the other ponies. Oddly enough it was Rose who was the touchy one. Instead of making for the bridge she tried to go down the riverbank.

"I'm *so* not getting covered in mud again," Jess said as she pulled hard on her reins. "Trot on, girl," she ordered firmly, and gentle Rose did as she was told.

When Jess had made it over the bridge, they all started to trot back towards the stables. But suddenly, as the ponies passed some trees near the bridge, Taffy whinnied loudly, stopped in his tracks and refused to move.

"Come on, boy," said Cara. But Taffy wouldn't budge.

Jess turned Rose round and came back to see what was going on. The other girls followed behind.

"What's wrong?" asked Jess.

"I don't know," said Cara. "He was fine on the bridge but now something's spooked him out."

"There must be something in the trees he doesn't like," said Amber.

"Shhhh," said Mel. "I can hear something."

The girls listened, and one by one they all heard the strange noise . . .

"It sounds like crying," said Cara. "I think someone's upset. We'd should go and see if they're OK."

The girls dismounted and led their ponies towards the trees. And they couldn't believe their eyes. Munching away at the grass in a small clearing was President, and sitting under a tree, covered in mud and bawling her eyes out, was Henrietta.

"Are you OK?" asked Cara kindly, kneeling down and putting her arm round Henrietta's shoulders. "Are you hurt?"

Henrietta looked up. "Oh, it's you lot. Just go away and leave me alone."

"Don't speak to Cara like that," said Mel crossly. "She was only trying to help."

"I don't *need* your help. I'm fine," said Henrietta.

"Well, you don't look it," said Jess. "Did you fall off at the bridge? It's really muddy down there and the ponies do get a bit scared."

Henrietta nodded.

"What were you doing down there anyway? You don't normally come out for a hack on your own," said Amber.

"If you must know, I was trying to find out what you lot were up to," said Henrietta. "All that whispering and giggling and the pink clothes. I knew you were planning something. And as soon as I get back I'm going to tell Vicki what you were doing when her back was turned."

"Tell her what you like," said Darcy. "She knows what we were up to. We took the ponies to see her at Sarah's wedding. And if you weren't such a sneak, Jess would have asked you too."

"I wouldn't have wanted to come anyway," said Henrietta.

"Oh, stop arguing. It doesn't matter," said Cara, who didn't like any sort of trouble.

"Cara's right," said Amber. "It's upsetting the ponies." And sure enough, they'd all stopped munching the grass and had laid back their ears.

"You'd better come back with us," Jess said to Henrietta. "Can you ride or are you too bruised?"

"I can ride," said Henrietta, feeling sorry for herself, "but President's quite spooked out and I can't catch him."

"Leave that to Amber," said Jess. "She'll be able to calm him down.'

A few minutes later Amber had caught President, and they all remounted their ponies and set off for the stables again.

By the time they were back in the yard it had turned cold and wet. The ponies were happy to be in their snug stables once more. After a good grooming they were given fresh water, a bucket of pony nuts and a net of sweet-smelling hay.

Henrietta called her father on her mobile and he came to get her. Without thanking the girls for helping her or saying sorry for spying on them, Henrietta just ordered them to groom President and then drove away with her nose in the air as usual.

"She's soooo rude," said Mel. "I can't stand her."

"She's not that bad," said Cara. "I feel sorry for her really. She's obviously got no friends."

"I'm not surprised," said Sam, and the others laughed.

When President had been groomed and fed, the girls set off for home. But before she left, Jess leaned over the stable door and listened to one of her favourite sounds in the world – Rose happily crunching pony nuts!

"Night-night, babe," she murmured softly.

Rose glanced up and whinnied at Jess, then turned back to her supper.

"Thanks for a fantastic day," Jess said. Then she smiled as she added, "Every day is a fantastic day just so long as I can be with you!"

Little Treasures

Little Treasures

"As long as you can ride a pony and follow clues, you'll be fine ..."

With the girls and their ponies all performing so well at her riding school, Vicki challenges them to try something different – a charity treasure hunt! All the girls are excited and hoping to win.

But snooty livery girl Henrietta is also desperate to come first, and when Cara and Mel find some surprise treasure during the hunt, it looks like she might just do that ...

Fancy Dress Ponies

Sam and her mum left the clown costume hanging over the stall and hurried to the tack room. They had no idea that someone had been listening in ...

It's the start of the summer holidays, and Sam and her friends are looking forward to spending as much time as they can at the stables. They decide to take part in a fancy dress competition, and work hard making themselves and their ponies look gorgeous.

But, as usual, stuck-up Henrietta is determined to spoil their fun. Is dressing up such a good idea after all ...?

Pony Club Weekend

"Life has to go on. You've got to start living. That's what Dad would have wanted."

Cara and the girls are taking part in a pony club weekend at Vicki's Riding School. For her friends, camping out, showjumping and competing in lots of races sound like fun. But this is the first time Cara's been away from her mum since her dad died and she's nervous about performing in front of everybody.

Will the weekend be as much fun as they hope? And will Cara get over her fears and enjoy it after all?